The Deductive Detective

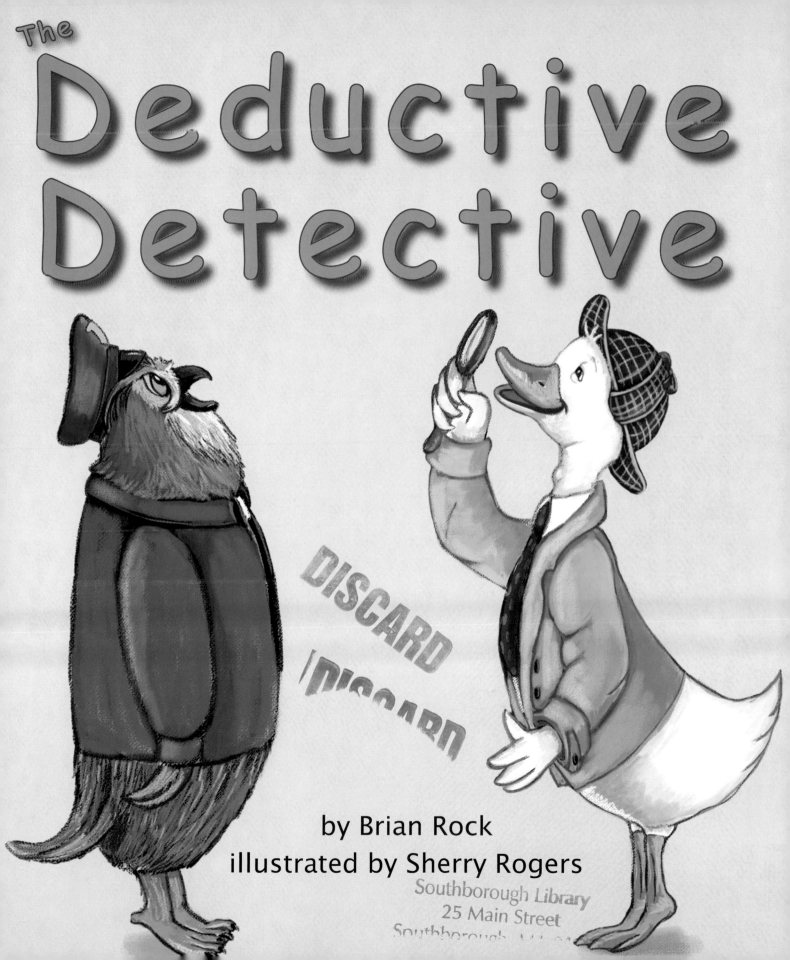

by Brian Rock

illustrated by Sherry Rogers

Duck, the deductive detective, was sitting at his desk when the phone rang with an urgent message: Someone stole one of the cakes from the cake contest!

Detective Duck is on the case!

When Duck arrived, Owl, the night watchman, took him to the scene of the crime. All thirteen bakers were already there. Fox was sitting in a chair crying, "Someone stole my beautiful cake!"

"*Hoo* could have stolen it?" asked Owl.

Detective Duck looked at the scene and said, "One of these twelve bakers stole that cake! But I'll quack this case in no time. I'll find clues that will subtract each suspect until there is just one left."

owl
pig
raccoon
swan
tiger

"Aha!" exclaimed Duck, pointing to the remaining cakes. "Look how small this cake is."

"That's my cake," squeaked Mouse. "I couldn't make a bigger cake or it would be too big for me to carry."

"And that is why you could not have stolen the cake," explained Duck.

"That," said Mouse "and because I only like cheesecake."

$$\begin{array}{r}
12 \text{ suspects} \\
\underline{-\ 1 \text{ mouse}} \\
11 \text{ suspects}
\end{array}$$

"Now," said Duck, "what time was the cake stolen?"
"It was taken at sunrise when I went to get breakfast," said Owl.

"That means you could not have taken the cake," said Duck, pointing at Rooster. "I heard you crow at sunrise this morning, so you could not have been here as well. So you're free to fly the coop."

"Great," said Rooster. "I've got other things to *cock a doodle do*."

11 suspects
- 1 rooster
10 suspects

"What about these doors?" asked Duck, pointing to the double doors at the front of the room. Were they still locked when the cake was stolen?"

"Of course, *hoo* else would have keys?" replied Owl.

"Then Elephant is not our thief," said Duck, "since the only way he can fit into this room is through these two doors."

"That's because I'm royalty," said Elephant. "I come from a long line of Tudors."

10 suspects
- 1 elephant
9 suspects

"And what's this?" said Duck as he looked closely at the table of cakes.

"It looks like a strand of hair," said Owl. "And look! There's some more over by the kitchen! *Hoo* could have left them?"

"Certainly not Swan," said Duck. "Swans have feathers, not hair. So Swan couldn't be our thief."

"Of course," said Swan. "The only thing I've ever stolen is the spotlight in *Swan Lake*."

9 suspects
- 1 swan
8 suspects

"It looks like our thief escaped through the kitchen," said Duck as he followed the strands of hair across the floor. "It looks dark in there. Have those lights been off all night?"

"Yes," answered Owl.

"But one of our suspects would never go into a dark room alone," said Duck, "which is why Horse is free to race home."

"It's true," said Horse. "I'm not a dark horse."

8 suspects
- 1 horse
7 suspects

Southborough Library
25 Main Street
Southborough, MA 01772

"Now let's shed some light on this case," said Duck as he opened the kitchen doors and turned on the lights. "Look at all those pots and pans hanging from the ceiling."

"*Hoo* knew we had so many pots and pans in here?" asked Owl.

"And not one of them has been knocked off, which means our big antlered friend Moose has not been through here lately."

"That's right," said Moose. "I haven't been here since I finished my chocolate moose cake."

7 suspects
- 1 moose
6 suspects

"Look, there on the floor," observed Duck.

"You mean that spilled flour?" asked Owl.

"Yes," replied Duck, "our thief spilled a bag of flour and dragged his long tail through it."

"But Pig doesn't have a long tail," said Duck, "so she couldn't have hogged the cake."

"I don't know why I even entered this contest," said Pig. "Nothing good ever happens when I'm bakin'."

6 suspects
- 1 pig
5 suspects

"The trail of flour leads here," said Owl, pointing to the counter.

"Which means whoever took the cake jumped up here before they left," explained Duck.

"But that's too high to jump," said Duck, "if you're a cow. So Cow is free to *moooo*-ve along home.

"I probably shouldn't mention this," said Cow, "but my great-grandmother once jumped over the moon."

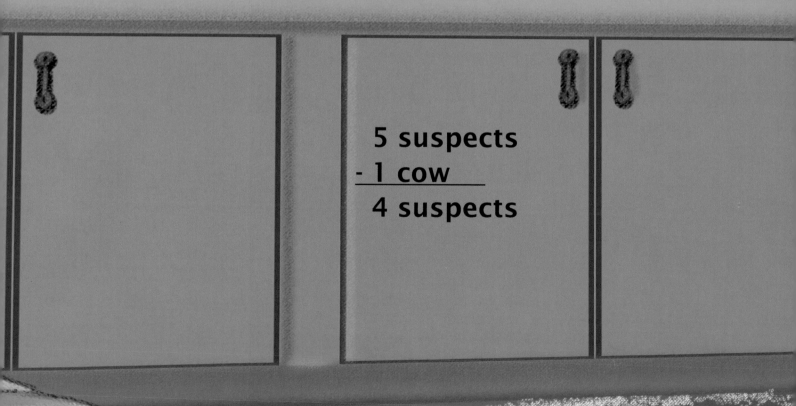

5 suspects
- 1 cow
4 suspects

4 suspects
- 1 tiger
3 suspects

"This window must be how he escaped," said Duck.

"*Hoo*?" asked Owl.

"The thief!" answered Duck. "And he left a handprint on the sill on the way out."

"This tells me that Tiger could not be our thief," said Duck, "because tigers have paws, not hands."

"And I have claws on my paws," said Tiger. "That's why I always bake from scratch."

"Look at that window," said Duck.

"What about it?" asked Owl.

"That's a pretty small space to crawl through," answered Duck, "especially if you're a kangaroo."

"Therefore Kangaroo is free to hop along home."

"Now I can go clean up," said Kangaroo. "My Joey's all doughy."

3 suspects
- 1 kangaroo
2 suspects

"Now where does the trail go from here?" asked Duck, looking out the window. "It's odd that there are no footprints on the ground," noticed Owl.

"Which means our thief must have swung from tree to tree to get away," said Duck.

"Which is very difficult to do," said Duck, "if you're a raccoon."

"Of course I'm the last suspect ruled out," said Raccoon. "Just because I have a mask everyone thinks I'm the thief."

"That means our thief could only be . . ."

$$\begin{array}{r} 2 \text{ suspects} \\ - 1 \text{ raccoon} \\ \hline 1 \text{ thief} \end{array}$$

"The Monkey!" said Duck pointing to the thief. **"The only question I have left is, why did you steal it?"**

"I couldn't help it," said Monkey, as Owl grabbed his arm. "It was a banana cream cake!"

For Creative Minds

Deductive Reasoning

Deductive reasoning is the term for answering a question by using facts and logic. Detective duck uses commonly known facts and logic to prove that some of the animals could not be the thief. For example: Detective Duck observes that the window the thief escaped through is small. He also knows that Kangaroo is much larger than the window. So he can logically prove that Kangaroo is not the thief!

You can be a detective too! Can you answer these questions and explain how you know the answers? Deductive reasoning is being able to explain why something is true by using facts. What are the facts that you used to answer the questions?

- If you are eating breakfast, what time of day do you think it is? Why?

- If it's dark and you turn on a light to see, is it day or night? Why?

- If you wake up to go to the bathroom and then go back to sleep, is it day or night? Why?

- If people are wearing raincoats and have wet umbrellas, what's the weather? Why?

- If you find a feather, did it come from a bird, mammal, or reptile? Why?

- If a wet towel is left in the girl's locker room, do you think a boy or girl left it? Why?

- If a cookie is missing and your little brother has cookie crumbs on his shirt, who do you think took the cookie? Why?

- If your little sister has a milk moustache, what do you think she was just drinking? Why?

- If you have air conditioning on in the house, do you think it is summer or winter? Why?

- If you are wearing a bathing suit and going to the beach to swim, what time of year is it? Why?

- If it is the last day of school for the year, what month is it? Why?

Compare and Contrast the Animals

Compare and contrast the animal suspects:

All birds have feathers. Which animals are birds?

Some animals are active at night and sleep during the day (nocturnal). Which animal is nocturnal?

Which animals fly, hop, and walk to move from one place to another?

Which animals have four legs?

Which animals use their front legs as arms and hands?

Which animal has a trunk?

Which animal has antlers?

Which animals have tails?

Which animals are big and which are little?

Which animals could you find on a farm?

Which animals might live in your backyard?

Which animals would you see in a zoo?

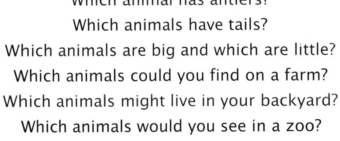

Birds: rooster and swan.   **Nocturnal:** raccoon   **Move:** Fly: rooster and swan; hop: kangaroo; walk: all others **Four legs:** cow, elephant, horse, kangaroo (the two front legs are short and are only used when moving slowly and eating or as arms), monkeys (like the kangaroo, monkeys use their two front legs for moving and as arms), moose, mouse, pig, raccoon, tiger   **Front legs as arms and hands:** kangaroos, monkeys and raccoons (who use their two front legs as arms).   **Trunk:** elephant   **Antlers:** moose   **Tails:** all but shape and length are all different   **Big:** cow, elephant, horse, kangaroo, moose, pig, swan (can be as big as an adult human), tiger   **Little:** monkey, mouse, raccoon, rooster **Farm:** cow, horse, pig, rooster   **Backyard:** mouse, raccoon, and maybe moose depending on where you live **Zoo:** elephant, kangaroo, monkey, moose, tiger